Casey Vice:

Spitfire of Vengeance

Joseph Rousell

CASEY VICE: SPITFIRE OF VENGEANCE

First edition. June 15, 2018.

ISBN: 978-1-948582-49-0

Written by Joseph Rousell.

Table of Contents

Prologue

August 1992

Casey Vice bit her lower lip and reached for her little sister's hand.

"No, LeAnn, the shoe is *mine*. Cameron is the iron, and you're the *hat*." She reminded her. She gently moved LeAnn's hand back to her own game token on the Monopoly board. "You have to move your *own* piece when you play this game."

Cameron, the eldest of the three, waited as Casey explained how the game worked for the fifth time. As their mother prepared dinner, the three children were camped out in the middle of the living room floor and doing their best to enjoy the game. It was still LeAnn's turn. She'd just rolled a 10 and reached for Casey's game piece instead of her own.

"But I want to be the shoe!" LeAnn whined, pouting her lower lip. "Why can't I be the shoe?"

"If you want to be the shoe, then you should've picked the shoe." Cameron said, as he pointed to her game token. "We let you pick yours first, and you picked the hat. Remember?"

LeAnn continued to pout as her two older siblings exchanged impatient looks. Casey blew out her breath and switched LeAnn's token on the board with her own.

"You actually fell for that, *again?*" Cameron mumbled. His brow furrowed with growing irritation, and he added, "Every time she does that, you give in and let her have whatever she wants."

Casey shook her head. "She's only five, Cameron. Just let her have the stupid shoe so we can keep playing!"

"Is everything okay in there?" their mother called from the kitchen.

"Yes!" Casey and her brother replied in unison. They both turned their attention to LeAnn, whose face lit up with a cherubic smile.

"Okay," Cameron grated. "Let's just get back to the game," he added, pointing to the shoe that now belonged to LeAnn. "Now you have to move ten spaces that way…"

Casey looked on as LeAnn counted the spaces out loud, landing on Park Place by the count of ten. Cameron reached for the dice to roll his turn, but the sound of a car pulling up to the front of his house froze his arm in mid-air.

Dad was home.

For as long as Casey could remember, everything came to a halt when their father came home from work. The way her brother explained it, their father was a very important man with a very dangerous job. Captain Richard Vice started a special police unit committed to taking down organized crime in their city.

As they waited eagerly for their father to walk through the front door, she heard another car pull up to the front of their house.

"Who is that?" Casey asked her brother, tugging at his gray pajama sleeve.

"I'm not sure," he answered, sitting up and turning towards the kitchen. "Mom! I think someone is outside with dad. Are we expecting company?"

"No," was all their mother said before she hurried out of the kitchen. She zipped past them towards the front of the house and shut the door behind her.

"Cameron, what's going on?" Casey asked her older brother. "Is company coming by?"

Cameron shook his head. "I don't think so. Mom always tells us if someone's coming over, so we can clean up first. But dad is home now, so it's probably nothing bad, right?"

A staccato bark of gunshots rang through the house, carrying their mother's horrifying screams with them as the front windows shattered in a hail of bullets. LeAnn screamed as the bullets hammered into the front door, through the living room, and into the wall behind them. Casey froze in terror, but her brother found the strength to move.

"Stay on your knees and follow me!" he shouted. Casey looked at him and forced herself to nod as he added, "Remember what dad taught us! We have to stay below the windows and crawl to the back of the house."

"The special room!" Casey yelled, trying to reach for LeAnn, who continued to scream in horror.

"No!" he blurted out, shaking his head at her. "I got LeAnn. Just follow me and remember to *stay down*."

Casey hesitated until she saw Cameron reach for LeAnn. She scrambled behind them as he led them toward the back of the house, straight to their father's panic room. Once they made it, Cameron cautiously opened the door, herding her and LeAnn into the room. After they were safely inside, he stood up, locked the door, turned on the lights, and motioned for them to get up off the carpeted floor.

There was a desk and a chair in the center of the room, and a sofa by the far-left wall. It also had a bathroom, a supply closet, and a weapon locker.

"There's the phone." Cameron said, walking over to the large brown desk.

Another barrage of bullets went off, this time from *inside* the house. Casey cringed from the terrifying sound, certain that her heart would jump out of her chest. LeAnn ran to the furthest corner of the room and continued to wail out in tears.

"Try to calm LeAnn down while I call 9-1-1!" Cameron shouted over the gunshots, wiping tears from his eyes as he pointed to their sister.

Casey sucked in several deep breaths, and then took off after her. Once she got hold of LeAnn, she pressed the palms of her hands against her sister's ears.

Her brother was on the line with the police dispatcher within seconds. In between his own sobs and sniffles, he explained what happened as best he could. Casey did her best to ignore the incessant gunfire, but she kept LeAnn's ears covered so at least *she* wouldn't have to hear any more of it.

* * *

"What's taking the police so long?" Casey asked, her voice trembling as she whispered.

"The responding officer is on his way, dear," the police dispatcher calmly assured them. "I'm going to stay on the line until he gets there. As long as you stay inside the room and keep the door locked, you'll be safe."

Casey looked around the room. Their father and their uncle built it in case of an emergency. Bulletproof plating had been installed underneath the sheetrock and door frame. The armored-plated door locked from the inside. All the windows were made of bulletproof glass. The supply closet held food, bottled water, a first-aid kit, a fire extinguisher, and bathroom supplies. The weapons locker held handguns from several different manufacturers, a dozen 12-guage shotguns, and fourteen rifles. Several drawers were built into the closet to store ammunition.

Two muffled voices, neither of which belonging to their parents, came through the walls from the living room. Casey smothered LeAnn's sobs with her shoulder, doing her best to keep her calm.

Cameron put the call on speaker and left the phone at the desk to sit on the floor just a few feet away from Casey and LeAnn. He readied himself to retrieve a weapon from the locker, until the dispatcher told him to leave the guns alone. She instructed him to keep the volume on the phone all the way up, so she could hear what was going on.

"We can hear two voices in the living room." Cameron explained, glancing at the phone before re-focusing on the door.

"Can you hear what they're saying?" the dispatcher asked him.

"Not yet," he said after a moment, tears welling in his eyes. Moments later, he whispered, "Wait! They just said something about police sirens down the street."

"That's the responding officer," the dispatcher's voice called over the speaker. "I told him that you're all in your father's panic room. Wait until Detective Burrell identifies himself before you open that door."

By the time Casey could hear the sirens, the intruders were already gone. Tears ran down her cheeks, but she wasn't sniffling or weeping like LeAnn. A sudden, hurried knock on the door startled them.

"Hello?" the officer called out. "This is Detective Mason Burrell, with the Saturn City Police Department."

"Yes, detective, we're here!" Cameron shouted.

"Cameron, is that you?" the detective asked. When they didn't answer right away, he asked, "Are you alright? Are any of you hurt?"

"No. But we're scared!" Casey yelled from across the room. "We're worried about our parents."

After a brief hesitation, the officer gently replied, "I understand that you're worried. Believe me. The bad men are gone. It's all clear out here now. EMS is standing by to check you over. Come on out and we'll get you all taken care of, okay?"

Her brother looked over to her as he stood up, nodded, and headed towards the door. Casey and LeAnn followed behind him as he unlocked the door and opened it.

"I'm glad to see you're all okay," Detective Burrell told them, turning towards the other officers in the house. "I've already called your uncle and your grandparents. They're on their way. Emergency Medical Services will examine you in the meantime."

"Our parents were outside when the shooting started," Cameron explained. He reached for LeAnn and picked her up. "Can't you at least tell us if they're okay?"

"The paramedics are doing everything they can to help them," he answered after a short pause.

"Why can't we just see our parents?" Casey asked. "Where are they? What happened to them?"

The detective got down on one knee, took a deep breath, and said, "I'm sorry, kids, but I think its best that we wait until your relatives arrive before I say anything else."

Casey was only eight years old, but she was the eight-year-old daughter of a police captain. She overheard enough of her father's conversations with her mother to understand what the detective was trying *not* to tell them. Her father had several conversations with her and Cameron in the past about children who lost their parents to gun violence.

She didn't need the officer to say it, because she already knew. Her parents weren't going to be okay. They weren't coming back inside to check on her or her siblings. She turned to her brother. She could tell from the look on Cameron's face that he knew, too.

Their mother and father were dead. She was never going to see them again.

Casey winced as LeAnn screamed in Cameron's arms.

"Where's my mommy?" LeAnn yelled, tears coursing down her face. "Where's my daddy? I want mommy and daddy!"

"We'll need to make arrangements for you to stay elsewhere," Burrell told them, doing his best to speak loud enough so that they could hear him over LeAnn. "Once your relatives get here, they can bring you down to the station, and then we'll…"

Casey couldn't hear the detective above LeAnn's screaming. The realization that their parents were dead sent a cold shiver through her entire body. She somberly gazed around the living room. The couches were overturned, and their Monopoly game was in shambles. There were several bullet holes in the walls, and a trail of bloodstained footprints led towards the front door. Most of the pictures that lined the walls were on the floor now, knocked down by the gunshots of the men who failed to kill them.

Cameron continued to console LeAnn. As Casey fought the urge to cry, one of the smaller pictures on the floor caught her attention. To her surprise, it wasn't broken. She walked over and picked it up. It was a family photo taken on Thanksgiving Day of the previous year. Another cold shiver went through her as she studied the image, and the frame slipped from her hand. She wasn't fast enough to catch it before it hit the floor, and watched as the glass shattered on impact.

Chapter 1

Fifteen Years Later

Casey cupped her hands underneath the warm water running from the bathroom sink. She tore her gaze away from the mirror long enough to wash up, then studied her reflection to check herself over. She'd repeatedly been hit on by men because of her light brown eyes, her flawless skin, and long red hair that ran past her shoulders. She never gave it any thought. The rugged cop she saw in the mirror didn't have time for a relationship. She didn't want one. She was married to her job. All she wanted out of life was to be a good detective *and* to find her sister, whom she hadn't seen in fifteen years.

A natural recluse, Casey valued personal space and grew up to be a workaholic who hated to take days off. She was only home now because her boss forced her to take a personal day. He believed she took her job too seriously for someone so young. She had too much of her father in her, he'd say. 15 years after his passing, she was still her father's daughter, carrying on the family business, as it were.

She enjoyed living alone in her spacious two-bedroom apartment. The furniture in her living room was simple but elegant, and affordable enough not to break the bank. Her sofa and two matching armchairs complimented the varnished floor. End tables on either side of the sofa and a matching coffee table in front of the couch completed the set.

On the wall behind her sofa were old family pictures her uncle salvaged from her childhood home. A flat-screen TV was mounted to the opposite wall. Casey rarely turned it on. Other than the news, she only cared to watch old sitcoms from the '80s. It was her way of remembering the good old days, before her family was torn apart.

Casey marched into the living room in pursuit of something to keep herself busy. She'd already cleaned her apartment. Other than watching television or reading a book, she was out of options. She headed towards the kitchen to make breakfast, but the telephone rang before she could reach the refrigerator. Casey ran to the living room in earnest to check the caller ID and smiled once she realized who was calling her.

"Cameron!" Casey squealed into the receiver with a giddy, melodic tone.

"Wow, you're actually home today?" Cameron replied in a deep but playful voice. "You're a hard one to keep in touch with. Don't tell me that the Spitfire of Vengeance finally decided to take a day off from beating the hell out of criminals!"

"My boss *made* me take a day off," she explained. She grinned as the words "Spitfire of Vengeance" echoed through her mind. "He feels that I take the job too seriously for my own good."

"He's right, you know," Cameron said. "It is good to hear from you, regardless. We haven't spoken in a month. I was getting worried!"

"I've just been busy, that's all." Casey replied. "You know how I am. I live for the job."

"Dad used to do that, too, you know?" Cameron replied. His voice took on a grim pitch as he continued. "Casey, you can't just bury yourself in work. Especially your kind of work. We lost our parents, *and* we lost LeAnn. I can't afford to lose you too."

Cameron never approved of her decision to join law enforcement. He always feared she would end up a target like their father. Her transfer to CIOC, the Criminal Intelligence/Organized Crime unit, only made things worse, because their father was the one who started the unit. Their sole purpose was to take the mafia head-on, and Casey relished every opportunity.

When she didn't respond, he added, "All I'm saying is that you're 23 years old. You have your whole life ahead of you.

Wait a decade or two before you bury yourself in work."

Casey thought about it for a moment, and replied, "Okay, I'll keep it in mind, but let's talk about why you really called. How are you doing on your end with the search for LeAnn?"

"About as good as you are," he answered her. "Which obviously translates to 'I've got squat' on my end."

Casey bit her lower lip and took several deep breaths. Over the last six years, she and Cameron spent an exhausting amount of time trying to find their sister to no avail. When their parents were murdered, the foster system immediately processed LeAnn because she was the youngest.

Carmichael, their father's brother, was given custody of Casey. Their mother's parents were given custody of Cameron. LeAnn was never seen or heard from again. It was as if she never existed. No digital fingerprint across the web. No school or hospital records. No phone number on record, no state ID on file anywhere in the country.

Just. Nothing.

Even with Cameron's position as Cape Foster's ADA, he and Casey's combined resources were insufficient to solve the mystery behind LeAnn's disappearance. It drove Casey to push even harder to find her, and Cameron's latest failed attempt was the last straw.

It also gave Casey an idea.

"We need some outside help," she finally said. "We need someone *really* good at finding people. I know someone who could look into this, as a favor to me."

"Don't even think about it!" Cameron snapped. "If this someone is your bounty hunter friend, then the answer is *no*. I don't want outsiders involved, especially Hamilton Lockwood."

"Dude, are you serious?" Casey shouted. "We've run into one dead end after another for the last six years! And Hamilton is my mentor, not some *outsider*! If he hadn't spent three years training me, I wouldn't be the cop that—"

A knock at her front door cut her off mid-sentence.

Who's at my door at seven o'clock in the morning? She thought to herself. Out loud, she said, "Hang on a second, there's someone at the door."

Casey looked through the peephole to see who deserved a kick in the junk. She dismissed the idea to follow through when she recognized the police badge.

"We'll have to finish our conversation later," she insisted, whispering over the phone. "My boss is at the door."

Cam hesitated. Then responded, "Yeah, that makes sense. I'm guessing he doesn't know about any of this?"

"Zilch," she replied sharply. "I'll talk to you later."

Casey ended the call as she opened the door and stood face to face with Mason Burrell. He was the captain of their unit. And he was the responding officer the night her parents were murdered.

"Detective," the large man said with a nod. "I apologize for coming by unannounced. I hope I didn't catch you at a bad time."

"You did, but I'll forgive the intrusion," Casey answered with a sarcastic grin. She stepped aside to let him in. "What brings you to my door this morning? You realized giving me the day off was a bad idea?"

"No, I'm glad I did," he answered plainly. He walked past her and headed towards one of the single chairs in the living room, and then took a seat as she closed the door behind him.

Captain Burrell was twice her age and twice her size. At six-one and two hundred pounds, he was in better shape than most of the younger officers on the force. Her five-five, one-hundred-thirty-eight-pound figure seemed flimsy compared to his, even though she was anything but. His rugged good looks came with a full head of dark hair that was slightly graying and a full beard that he kept well-groomed. His blue eyes were cold and serious, even when he was happy.

Casey could tell that he was anything but happy as he waited for her to join him. She quickly made her way over to the couch and took a seat.

"It isn't often that my captain drops by while I'm in my pajamas," she said. "I haven't had breakfast yet, but you're welcome to–"

"Cassandra, I'm here to warn you," Burrell replied before she could finish. Whenever he called her Cassandra instead of Casey, something *very* serious was on his mind. "You received a call at HQ less than an hour ago. Since you're out for the day, I had the call transferred to my desk. The call came from the residence of Shawn Anderson. He left a personal invitation to his mansion at *your* earliest convenience."

Casey responded with a bemused look.

Shawn Anderson, known by his nickname "The Jackknife," was the biggest crime boss in the city. He was a sybaritic despot who ruled the criminal underworld. For over a decade his influence spread through Saturn City like a virus, and his hatred for the CIOC unit wasn't a secret. It spearheaded the war against the criminal underworld and slowly forced his influence to wane. Now *she* was on the radar of Saturn City's kingpin.

"Why would he call me?" she asked him, only mildly surprised. "I want nothing to do with him, aside from making his existence painful every chance I get."

"That's why *I personally* delivered this message," Burrell replied, shaking his head as he took note of the obvious satisfaction in her voice. "I have no idea *why* he called, but it can't be good."

Casey nodded in agreement and made note of the genuine concern in his voice. From the day she officially joined the force, Mason kept an extremely close eye on her. He was ultimately the reason she was promoted after being on the force for only three years. Although, her accomplishments as a beat cop did help *a lot*. The promotion itself was the only way she could be assigned to the CIOC unit. From his perspective, bringing her into the unit that her father founded was a fitting way to honor his legacy.

"I don't like this, Cassandra," he continued. "Everyone in this city knows you follow in Richard's footsteps and even as a rookie your career was heavily publicized. But when you break the jaw of a registered level-three sex-offender for cornering an adolescent in a parking lot, that's what happens."

"I'm fighting to clean up this city, like my father did when he was alive," Casey replied, although she was saying it more to herself than to him. "The way I see it, it was just a matter of time before Anderson's path eventually crossed mine."

"The matter isn't open for consideration, Vice." Captain Burrell shook his head, and sighed. He got up and headed towards the front door, and she followed behind to let him out. He turned to her and added, "You've got enough sense to realize this is bad. Shawn Anderson will kill you without blinking an eye. And don't get me started about Internal Affairs! A kingpin sends a personal invitation to the most publicly recognized member of a unit devoted to ending organized crime? Social visit or not, do you have *any idea* what IA would do to *us* if you *did* go? *Especially* if *you* end up *dead*?"

Of course I do! Casey's eyes met his, but she didn't respond. *For starters, we would both get the ax. And that's if I don't get killed!*

"This is one time where I hope you'll be smart enough to put that maverick spirit of yours in check," Burrell told her. "As your boss," he hesitated briefly, and then added, "and as your friend, I want you to promise me you won't do anything stupid."

Casey could only smile in response as she reached for the doorknob. Of course, Casey *wasn't* stupid. She wasn't going to do anything that would deliberately put her boss or anyone else that she cared about in jeopardy.

But I can't just ignore the feeling that there's something more to this invitation.

"I'll behave myself," Casey finally said before adding, "And besides, if he were *smart*, he wouldn't invite me to his house, so clearly Shawn Anderson isn't the brightest bulb in the chandelier."

Casey closed the door before he could respond. She headed back toward the couch to ponder whether she should pass on Anderson's invitation. Why reach out to her a year after she joined the CIOC? Someone like him wouldn't invite *her* into his home without an agenda. So, what was it?

Chapter 2

It's too late to turn back now.

Casey pulled her vehicle up to the intercom mounted to the fence post.

"Identify yourself, Miss," growled an unfriendly voice from the speaker.

The single security camera two feet above it caught her eye.

It's too late to turn back now.

"This is Casey Vice," Casey replied. "I'm here via personal invitation from Shawn Anderson."

Silence. Then the unfriendly voice replied, "Confirmed. Standby, *Detective*. Bring your vehicle into the garage on the right. Someone will meet you there."

Damn, what did I ever do to you? she thought, before reprimanding herself. *Oh yeah, I'm an off-duty cop from a special unit that makes your life miserable. And I'm here to see your boss. Yeah, I get it now.*

Five hours had passed before Casey decided to accept the

invitation. Now she felt like she had made a terrible mistake. But it was too late to turn back now.

Casey wore a green blouse, black dress slacks, black leather boots and a black leather jacket. Her hair was tied back in a ponytail and she wore very little makeup. She chose not to wear a wire on the chance she'd be searched, but she kept her Ruger P95PR holstered to the right side of her waist. Social call or not, it never hurt to be prepared if things took a bad turn.

A few seconds later, the gate opened. Casey drove onto the estate and backed into the garage located on the right side of the house. A well-groomed man dressed in a gray leisure suit came out of the house, accompanied by two women. They approached her as she got out of her car.

The large, well-built man stood over six feet tall and weighed at least three hundred pounds. Casey noticed he wasn't armed. But the two women were. Both were roughly the same age and size as Casey. The one on the left was a little taller than the other. It took a moment for her to realize they were all smiling as they approached.

"Good afternoon, Miss Vice," the large man said in a suspiciously pleasant voice. "My name is Wyatt. I'm the head of security here at the mansion and Mr. Anderson's second in command. It's a pleasure to finally meet you in person."

He held his massive right hand out for a handshake. Cautiously, and with just a hint of reluctance, Casey extended her own hand to oblige him.

Wyatt gestured to the two women and said, "This young lady to my left is Danielle, and the woman to my right is Yovanni. They're two of Anderson's personal enforcers, the very best he has under his command."

Casey studied the Jackknife's lieutenant and his two personal bodyguards. Both women were dressed in black collared blouses with short sleeves and black jeans cut low, with black combat boots. They both carried two guns identical to her own, holstered to either side of their waists. She also noticed they both had a can of mace strapped to their right side, and a baton strapped to their left thigh.

Despite their "pleasant" disposition, the three clearly meant business.

"It's nice to meet you both," Casey said, trying her best to not sound insincere.

She stepped forward to extend a handshake to Danielle first. The woman remained silent, but she did shake Casey's hand. Danielle was the quiet type; Casey could tell that much from studying her body language. A woman of action and very few words, she had olive-toned skin, long dark hair and dark eyes that were forbidding.

"Likewise, Detective Vice," Yovanni said to her, extending a handshake of her own.

Casey shook Yovanni's hand as she sized her up. She was the prettier one. Casey assumed she did most of the talking between the two of them. She was also the most dangerous. Danielle's personality was very straight-forward and much easier to read. Yovanni's curly brown hair, sharply accentuated features, hazel eyes and warm skin tone made her a wolf in sheep's clothing. Casey figured Yovanni could sweet-talk almost anyone into dropping their guard if they weren't careful.

Fortunately, Casey had no intention of dropping her guard around any of them.

"We were tasked by Mr. Anderson to bring you directly to him when you arrived," Wyatt said, maintaining his pleasant smile as he pointed to Casey. "Since we're on a tight schedule, we'll have to skip the vehicle inspection. But you'll have to keep it parked in the guest garage. It'll be safe there. You have my word."

"I suppose that'll be fine," she answered him. *I'll have to remember to inspect my car before I leave,* she thought to herself. "So," she asked out loud, "why did your boss invite me here?"

Wyatt shook his head. "We're under orders not to say. He wants to speak with you in private. So, shall we?"

Casey nodded and followed behind Wyatt as he led the way. Danielle and Yovanni quietly followed one step behind her.

"This European-style, two-story structure is over thirty years old," Wyatt explained to her, as he opened the front door. Stretching his arms out to his sides, he added, "It's has four bedrooms, five bathrooms, two garages, a living room, and a dining room, a separate room for eating breakfast…"

Who cares? Casey thought to herself. As she a got close-up of Anderson's mansion, it was clear to her that he enjoyed the finer things in life, no matter the cost. She nodded in mock approval as he spoke, keeping a smile on her face to sell the act. Her skills as a trained observer kicked in while she tuned him out. She eyed the mini-camera above the front door. As she gazed up at the chandelier hung smack in the center of the foyer, she noticed it also housed another camera. Casey filed the info away in her memory as she followed him towards the staircase to the left.

Another camera caught Casey's attention as they made it to

the top of the stairs, lodged in a lighting fixture next to one of the rooms. The door to the room stood out to her, as if she'd seen one like it before. A cold shiver came over her when she realized why— it looked almost identical to the door of her father's old panic room. If she was right, the door was reinforced to keep intruders and bullets from getting in. Once the door was locked, nothing short of explosives would open it.

"Is *that* where you're taking me?" Casey asked, pointing to the room.

"That's the boss's office, and its off limits," Wyatt answered. There was a hint of reluctance in his tone as he added, "*We* don't even have access to that room. No one is allowed in there unless the boss is with them."

"Uh-huh," She replied, nodding in compliance. *So, he has an office with a reinforced door, like my dad's panic room? I'm getting more and more bad vibes about this visit.*

Wyatt redirected Casey's attention away from Anderson's office to a set of double doors. "Our destination is *this* way, Detective," he said.

Casey followed him into what looked like a built-in diner. From her vantage point, there wasn't anything special about the diner itself, but on the other side were two sets of double-doors.

"That's where you're headed," Yovanni pointed out. "The city's skyline is visible from the terrace. It's his favorite place in the entire mansion."

"I can see why," Casey replied.

The terrace didn't just overlook the backyard of the estate. More than half of Saturn City's commerce district could be seen in the distance. Casey stepped through the doors and was immediately drawn to the same awe-inspiring view that kept the mansion's owner in a trance. The forceful thud of the double-doors closing snapped them both out of it.

Anderson turned to face her for a split second before resuming his view. Casey looked behind her to see that Wyatt and the two enforcers were gone, leaving her and Shawn Anderson by themselves. And for the first time in her life, Casey Vice finally got to meet Saturn City's crime lord. He was as tall as Captain Burrell and in his early fifties at least. He had graying short-brown hair and a broad face. His green eyes were bright and narrow, and his gold watch probably cost more than her annual salary.

"I've been following your career for a while now, Detective," he said, still peering out at the skyline in the distance as he spoke. "I'm honored to finally meet the infamous Casey Vice face-to-face."

"Are you really?" she asked, ignoring his insincere snort. She cautiously walked up to him and added, "I'm under the impression you want me dead, considering my line of work. It makes me even more curious about why you called me."

She let the question hang between them.

"What do you think of my home?" Shawn finally asked, turning his body halfway to face her.

"I didn't see much of it," she admitted. When he remained silent, she locked eyes with him. *He's got the glare of a snake and the posture of a peacock,* she thought. *Typical for a sociopath.* She observed him for a moment. "The way Wyatt kept going on about it," she began, "you'd think it were for sale."

"You've been a busy woman, Detective Vice." Shawn admitted, making no attempt to hide his admiration. "Throughout the short time you've been on the force, the media has been on fire about the waves you've made. You've taken down rapists, drug dealers, and wife-beaters, to name a few. But you make life complicated for those of us who make our living the *non-traditional* way."

"You didn't call me here hoping for an apology, did you?" she asked with a mild hint of sarcasm in her voice. "Because if you did—"

"In just a few years you earned a spot in the most prestigious task force in the city," he interrupted. "Do you realize how *visible* a target you are? Many in the criminal underworld want your head on a plate, Detective. Fortunately for *you*, I run a *very* tight ship."

This is where a wire would've come in handy! Casey thought to herself. *And I can't use my phone to record him without him noticing. I should've turned it on beforehand! Dammit!*

"I hold great influence in this city, the likes of which the common man can only dream about." Anderson continued with a straight face. "But my authority isn't absolute; you are proof of that, as is the rest of your unit. Captain Burrell is a serious thorn in my side, but *you*, Cassandra Vice…" He paused briefly, and then asked, "May I call you that, or do you prefer Casey?"

Casey tilted her head to the side and shrugged. *Just make your frickin' point! Spit it out already!*

"I'll come to the point, Cassandra," he began again. "I realize you and I are at cross-purposes, and I want to change that. I admire what you've accomplished in such a short time, but it's nothing compared to what you could achieve if you worked *with* me rather than *against* me. *That's* why I called you here today. I want you to be my eyes, ears and voice in the CIOC unit."

Casey's jaw dropped. *Really?! That's why you wanted to meet me? Dude, are you high, or are you just stupid?!*

"Thanks, but *no thanks*," Casey answered him, once the initial shock wore off. She shook her head. "My soul isn't for sale, Mr. Anderson. So, if there's nothing else...."

The two of them stared each other down in silence, studying one another. Anderson wasn't smiling anymore. *There's that sociopathic glare again*, she noted. The hairs on the back of her neck stood on end, but she refused to look away.

A second later, he turned away from her, his gaze once again fixed on the skyline.

"You know, your dad and I went way back," he finally said without turning to face her, his voice suddenly less friendly. "As I rose in the ranks of organized crime, we crossed paths several times. He made life as difficult for me as you have. Eventually, the head of the family told me I needed to prove myself. He gave me the responsibility of dealing with your father.

"I offered him the same opportunity as you." He continued. "I gave him a chance to work with me to avoid eliminating him. But your father was a stubborn and principled man. He started the CIOC unit specifically to take down the mob. When the order finally came down from the Don, I had a choice to make: my life, or your fathers. I made every effort to avoid putting out a hit on him."

Casey's heart almost stopped beating in her chest. *Did he just say…?*

"I hope you'll avoid making the same mistake and *accept* my offer," he said with a grin. "Just this once, *don't* follow in your father's footsteps."

Her chest numbed as she put all the pieces together— the immense anxiety she felt when she accepted his invitation, his people being so nice to her, the door to his private office. It wasn't a coincidence that it reminded her of her dad's old panic room. The same panic room that saved her life the night her parents were murdered.

It was a sign. He's the one. He may not have been the one shooting the bullets, but Shawn Anderson is the reason my parents are dead.

It made sense *now* why her parents' killers were never found, the case never solved. She finally knew *who* was responsible, and now he'd threatening to have her killed, too. Casey's left eye twitched, her jaw tightened, and she swallowed hard. It took all her self-control to fight the urge to pull out her gun and shoot him in the face.

NO! You can't afford to lose it, especially since you shouldn't even be here. She spotted the security camera in the corner. *And you can't arrest him, because it's you, by yourself, against him, his top three bloodhounds, and God knows who else that you didn't see. Think, dammit! Testimony without hard proof might work for the ADA, but he'll probably want the security recording. Now rein yourself in, or else you won't get out of here alive.*

"Careful, Detective," Anderson mocked, pointing to the same camera. "My people are watching. Besides, you aren't wired, and the only evidence of our meeting will be in my possession. You can't prove *anything*."

"That won't stop me," she hissed through clenched teeth. "You have no idea what I'm capable of. Mark my words: I'll bury you for what you've done."

"Then I suppose we're done here, Miss Vice," he replied casually. As the doors to the terrace flew open, he concluded, "You should really watch that temper of yours, by the way. It's not good for someone your age to be so angry."

Wyatt walked out onto the terrace and approached her. Casey

quickly glanced in his direction and saw that he was alone and still unarmed, but his expression was cold and unwelcoming.

Casey turned her attention back to Anderson and said, "Proof or no proof, my temper is the least of your problems. This isn't over between you and me."

Anderson laughed and gave her a dismissive handwave as he turned away.

Casey spun angrily on her heels to head for the terrace exit. She marched through the diner and headed down the center staircase as Wyatt quietly followed. Casey was uncertain whether he would attack her, but she kept a tightened grip on her gun just in case. Once she finally made it to the front door she turned to face him. He still had a cold, grim look across his face. Without a word, Casey shook her head and turned to leave.

Chapter 3

Casey thoroughly inspected her vehicle before she left Anderson's estate. To her surprise, it hadn't been tampered with. But it was only a matter of time before he moved to eliminate her. Without the recording from the surveillance feed, she had nothing but her word to go on. It would make matters worse if she suddenly turned up dead. Anderson could destroy the evidence to cover himself, leaving no concrete proof of the encounter. It would be as if the meeting never happened in the first place.

Still, she couldn't let it go, especially after she just painted a bull's-eye on her back. During their confrontation, she realized Anderson was used to always being in control. The way he expected her to approve of his lavish mansion. The glare of disapproval to her general indifference to him. His cavalier recollection of ordering her father to be murdered. And his flippant dismissal of her response, when he pointed to the camera recording his confession. A man of his inflated self-esteem would rather die than go to jail, and from his perspective, he had all the leverage.

It was inevitable; one of them *was* going to die in the end.

So help him God, I'm gonna put that cocky ignoramus in the ground!

Casey pulled up to her apartment building, grabbed her phone and dialed Captain Burrell at his desk. As one-sided as the situation might have seemed, it made sense to let him know what happened. When he didn't pick up, she considered trying his cell once she made it to her apartment. With her life in immediate peril and no time to waste, Casey burst through the front doors of her apartment complex. She bolted for the elevator at the far end of the hall. When the elevator made it to the ground level, she threw herself inside and pressed the button for her floor.

Just as she'd hoped, the elevator was vacant. There were also no security cameras inside. For two years she complained to the owner of the building about it, until she nearly turned blue in the face.

She shook her head. *Money-hoarding cheapskate! You own a multimillion-dollar apartment complex, and you won't even spare a thousand dollars for surveillance cameras. Even after I offer to set them up for FREE!*

When the elevator reached her floor she almost broke into a run. She was within 12 feet of her apartment when she noticed the front door was kicked in.

She immediately reached for her gun and inched closer to her apartment. She could hear a man and a woman's voice drift through the doorway, their hushed voices urgent and threatening. Casey quietly snuck inside, her weapon aimed at the backs of the two intruders standing in her living room.

"Freeze!" Casey shouted. "Hands up where I can see them and turn around. Now!"

Once they turned around to face her, she gave each of them a good look-over. There was a vicious spark in their eyes, especially the woman. Neither of them appeared to be armed, which she found a little strange. Just as she'd anticipated, Anderson wasted little time making good on his threat.

Seriously, though? Stereotypical mafia muscle hired to make my death look like an "accident?" So damn tactlessly cliché it's sickening! You could at least be a little more original! Jackass!

The woman took a breath and said, "Good afterno—"

"Shut up!" Casey aimed the gun at the woman's chest. She kept the man within her line of sight in case he moved, and asked, "Which one of you *geniuses* thought it was a good idea to break into my home?"

They both remained silent.

"Answer me, dammit!" Casey snapped. Her full red lips formed a vicious snarl and she tightened her grip on her weapon.

"Here's the abridged version, Detective," the man said menacingly, indifferent to the fact that her gun was now pointed at *his* chest. "You've pissed off the wrong people for the last time. There's a million-dollar bounty on your head, and we're here to collect."

Casey's left eye twitched violently as her feelings egged her on: *Shoot em' in the damn head, already! You need to send a message to that asshat for what he's done! Teach him–and everyone else–not to cross you! Kill these two morons, and—*

An inhumanly powerful hand clenched the back of her neck.

Casey's curved figure flew weightlessly across the living room, towards the kitchen. She hit the ground hard with a loud thud, gasping for air. When she finally made it to one knee, she sized up the man who'd tossed her aside like yesterday's trash. He was even larger than Wyatt, dressed in black from head to toe.

How did I not hear this overstuffed biscuit sneak up behind me?! She struggled to ignore the rapid throbbing of her own heartbeat. *And I managed to lose my gun. I've really stepped in it this time! Lockwood would flog me to death if he were here.*

Granted, he'd kill these three in less than two seconds, and then he'd flog me to death!

"You should've taken the bosses offer, kid," the large man said with a deep voice. Flanked by both of his accomplices, he pointed *her gun* at her head. "Now I get to bury another badge at the bottom of the river. We were supposed to avoid shooting you to make it look like an accident. But hey, a million dollars is a million dollars. Right?"

Casey cautiously raised her hands when she noticed Captain Burrell standing in her doorway, with two officers on either side of him. All three officers' guns were aimed at the larger man's back, and opened fire before he could pull the trigger. The man dropped to his knees before he fell forward, his grip on Casey's weapon loosened as he lay there motionless.

As their accomplice lay dead at their feet, the two other intruders stood mortified. Their eyes fell to their partner's body and then to the officers who shot him. Casey relished the fear on their faces.

Sick 'em!

Casey leapt at the two with a snarl, more animalistic than human. She thrust her shin forward into the man's groin. He fell to his knees, his hands lowered to his crotch to cover up. A solid right hook to his temple dropped him to the ground. Then she rushed the woman with a swift uppercut to the gut. A vicious head-butt on the chin knocked the woman out cold.

High on adrenaline and breathing heavily, Casey turned her attention to the body of the man who tried to shoot her with her gun. She retrieved it from his lifeless grip and then stepped over his corpse to address her rescuers.

"Thanks for the assist," she said to them with a nod. She immediately recognized the two detectives with Captain Burrell. Jonathan Muldoon and Giselle Sosa were both members of the CIOC. Casey wiped a bead of sweat from her forehead, and said, "I'm surprised to see you, since I never reached you at your desk."

"Yeah, because I'd already left to come here," he began to explain with a low, threatening growl. He nodded to the intruders. "The station got an anonymous call about a break-in at this address. I personally responded, because I remember what happened this morning."

"He brought us with him just to be on the safe side," Giselle added, as she holstered her gun and reached for her handcuffs.

"I *decided* to keep things in the *family*," Burrell corrected. "Officers from our own unit were the obvious choice. I picked

Giselle and Jonathan because the three of you are friends.

"Now, as I recall," he continued, "I stopped by early this morning to inform you of a personal invitation from Shawn Anderson. For whatever reason, he invited you to see him at his estate. And as your *Captain*, as your *friend*, I trusted *you* to make the *sensible* choice *not* to go! I believed you would consider the consequences we'd have to face, *if* you didn't get *killed* outright! But let me guess. You completely ignored me and went anyway, didn't you?"

Casey's mouth formed into a frown, and she nodded. Their eyes locked, and all she could see in them were bold, blue flames hot enough to roast flesh from bone. Casey's heartbeat sped up again.

"And what would you have done if he tried to kill you outright?!" Burrell snapped. His voice bounced off the walls of Casey's door-less apartment. She flinched in response. "You went behind my back! Do you know what Internal Affairs could do to our unit? Do you know what they can do to *you* if they think *you're* crooked? Everything we've accomplished? Down the drain! I should suspend you for six months without pay!"

"I won't try to explain or justify my actions away," Casey said. Her voice was calm, her hands raised. "But I screwed up bad, Captain. You have every right to be pissed at me, and—"

"You didn't think things through, Cassandra! *That's* why I'm pissed at you!" Burrell barked. "What would I tell Cameron if you got murdered? How would I tell your uncle or grandparents? Dammit, Vice! You're *smarter* than this! You should *know* better!"

Casey froze. Giselle and Jonathan watched with wide eyes; neither one intervened. Captain Burrell rarely showed anger towards her, and he never raised his voice at *anyone*. Until now, he never *needed* to. Casey knew better than to utter so much as a word.

She was wrong. *Dead* wrong.

"Hey, Cap! I recognize this guy," Jonathan said. Everyone's attention turned to him, and he pointed at the dead body of the man who tried to shoot Casey. "He's an enforcer for the mob who goes by the name 'Tiny.' He's one of the suspected cop killers we've been investigating for the past two years."

"Well, he's *dead* now!" Casey spit out with as much venom as she could muster. "He admitted to killing cops *and* that he worked for the Jackknife. So do the two of them. They mentioned a one-million-dollar bounty on my life."

"Cassandra, what the hell happened?" Burrell asked. His voice was less threatening now, but no less serious. He glanced at the two unconscious perpetrators, returned his attention to her, and added, "Start at the beginning. Don't leave *anything* out. I want to know *everything*."

Casey took a deep breath and nodded. "I can do that."

While Giselle and Jonathan cuffed the two unconscious intruders, Casey told the three of them about the meeting with Anderson. She explained how he offered her a job working for him as the mole in their unit, and that he admitted to having her father killed for refusing a similar offer fifteen years ago.

"Damn it! That explains a lot," Burrell finally said once she was done. "When he doesn't hear back from these three idiots, he'll know they've probably botched the job. We've got to move fast."

"So what's the plan?" Casey asked, her eyes widened with excitement. "We finally gonna nail him to the wall?"

"The *plan* is that you are going to *disappear*," he answered her plainly. "You've done enough already, getting yourself in this mess. We'll handle this."

Casey's wide-eyed eagerness turned into a narrow-eyed glare. "Say what?"

"You heard me right," he assured her. "You're lucky *enough* to still be alive, *Cassandra*. For your own sake, I want you as far away from this as possible, so you're leaving the city. As of now you are officially on vacation. Once we clean up here and you're out of reach, I'm opening an investigation for the attempt on your life. And I'm bringing Anderson in."

"I'm not going on vacation after someone tried to murder me!" Casey snapped. "Boss, this should be *my* case. He had my father killed. He tried to have *me* killed, so I should be the one to take him down."

"When you say you're going to 'take him down', do you mean you're going to bring him in?" Burrell asked her, "Or do you mean you're gonna put a bullet in his head?"

"That's what happens when the mob puts a million-dollar hit on my life." Casey told him, nodding. "As long as he's alive to pay whoever is stupid enough to try to collect, I can't run from this."

"If you won't follow my orders, hand over your badge and your gun. Now." he demanded. His gruff voice echoed in the apartment. "*You* shouldn't have gone to see Anderson in the *first place*. You should be grateful to still have your job, *Maverick*! You're not using this as self-justification to murder a man in cold blood. Believe me, I can empathize with how you feel. I was there with you and your siblings that night. Richie Vice was my father figure long before I joined the force, when I didn't have a dad of my own. So, trust me when I tell you, I understand."

"Then you should understand *why* I have to finish this," she countered. She could taste the defiance on the tip of her tongue as she added, "I'll turn in my badge and my gun, if that's what it takes. But I'm going after him, even if I gotta do it by myself. The Jackknife is as good as dead."

Burrell shook his head as they stared each other down. He knew Casey wasn't making an idle threat. She had a big mouth, but she could back it up. The Jackknife tried to have her murdered and failed. Casey would respond with swift and extreme prejudice, and no one would be able to stop her.

"So rather than protect you from the mob, I need to protect you from yourself?" Burrell asked her. "We're gonna go down this route, Vice?"

Casey didn't answer him. The fire in her eyes was enough of a yes for him to know she was forcing his hand. Arms crossed, she bit her lower lip and held his gaze.

After a long period of uncomfortable silence, he finally said, "Okay, this is the plan." His blue eyes shifted to the two mafia grunts, both of whom were just starting to move. "Jonathan, I want you and Giselle to call it in so they can send a coroner for the body. Take these two suspects in for processing and start the paperwork the moment you get there. Charge them both with attempted capital murder. And don't say a word to anyone else until I get there. Captain's orders.

"I'll talk to the commissioner personally," he continued. "He'll get the wheels turning for an arrest warrant. We will both need to give a statement to the Judge for him to approve it, because of our *unique* situation. Cassandra, you'll have to include every detail about the meeting with Shawn Anderson, no matter how incriminating it looks. If we do have to deal with Internal Affairs, the naked truth will help us more than well-dressed lies."

"A confession from these two would move things along," Casey insisted. She turned to her attackers and flashed them a devious glare. Both of them winced in response. She nodded with satisfaction, and added, "Put me in a room with them, and I'll get it for you. I guarantee it."

"Not a chance," Burrell countered. "You've had enough action for now. Get your house in order after the coroner removes the stiff. Save your energy for the operation. In the meantime, I'll put surveillance on Jackknife's estate, and a police tail on *him* until we get the green light. When it's time to move in, I'll assemble the entire CIOC unit, and a 20-man SWAT team. So, if you want a shot at the Jackknife, you're going to do it *my* way. And *that's* my final offer. Take it or leave it."

Casey opened her mouth to respond. Nothing came out. If she wanted to see Anderson pay *and* keep her job, she had to concede.

She *had* to.

When she nodded, Burrell sighed in relief and said, "Okay, good. Now that *that* fire is out, let's move.

Chapter 4

Seven. Five. One.

Seven. Five. One.

Seven. Five. One.

Casey planted herself on the sofa, pressed her palms down on the top of her thighs, squared her shoulders and shut her eyes. Her stomach was in knots and her muscles twitched every few seconds. Her heartbeat was rapid and her mouth was dry. She pressed her tongue against the roof of her mouth, inhaled deeply for seven seconds, held for five and then exhaled quickly. Within a couple of minutes, she could swallow again, and her heartbeat returned to normal. Several minutes after, the twitching ceased, but she continued with the exercise.

Seven. Five. One. Seven. Five. One. Seven. Five. One.

It was the first of five exercises she learned from Lockwood before she joined the force. It was also her favorite because it was the easiest to do.

Always count to yourself as you inhale, hold and exhale. He used to tell her during their training sessions. *Counting will redirect you from your emotions. You can regain control with logic, and this exercise will be a good start. Seven. Five. One. Seven. Five. One. Seven. Five. One. Seven. Five. One…*

Two hours passed since the attempt on Casey's life. Jonathan and Giselle were at the station, and the two perpetrators were in custody. The coroner wrapped up and removed Tiny's corpse from the apartment. Burrell stayed behind to take her statement and then stepped into the hallway to call the Commissioner. Every so often, Casey opened her eyes and caught him watching her. After what she'd done, she didn't blame him. Their careers were on the line if this operation tanked. And despite her actions, he was still willing to stick his neck out on her behalf. She *had* to make sure he didn't regret it.

"Okay, this is what I've got." Burrell said, as he clapped his hands. The echo thundered across the living room of her door-less apartment. "It'll be another three hours before the arrest warrant reaches the judge. Since it's for attempted capital murder, the commissioner will shave as much time off as he can. He's already putting the S.W.A.T team together for me. They'll be ready to go once the warrant is in our hands."

Casey closed her eyes and took a deep breath. "What else did he say?"

"Well, Internal Affairs *isn't* going to hang us," Burrell said.

Casey's eyes snapped open. "Cap, are you for real?"

Burrell shrugged. "The commissioner cursed me out for telling you about the invitation, but that's all. In his own words, this is just as much *my* fault. He knows you're too honest to turn crooked. But he said I should've come to *him* with it, not *you*. Fortunately for us, between Anderson's invitation, the tip-off about the break-in, the dead cop killer, the two mutts in custody, and our statements, he thinks we've got enough for a righteous warrant for an attempted capital murder. And once we apprehend Anderson, we can re-open the investigation into your parents' deaths."

Casey's mouth flew open.

"For now, I want you to stay here," he told her. "I've been watching you, kid. You *need* time to screw your head on straight." He gestured around her apartment. "There's more than enough here to keep you occupied. That's *all* I want you to do. Once you're in a better headspace, come to the station. When we take down the Jackknife, I expect you to be at your best."

Casey nodded. "I'll call the super for the building. He can replace the door for me while I clean up. But there's still the matter of a million-dollar hit that—"

"I'm already way ahead of you," he cut her off. "Since you're stubborn and *refuse* to leave, I got authorization to post a heavily armed police guard at this complex. They'll cover every entrance to this building, every floor and every stairwell. I personally cleared everyone assigned to this detail, especially the ones outside your door. I handpicked people *we* can trust."

"That's comforting," Casey admitted, "since I'd hate to rely on you to come to my rescue again. But for real, I owe you one. Regardless of what the Commish said, I know I put you in a bad spot. I apologize for being such a damn fool."

"Don't kick yourself in the ass too hard!" Burrell nodded with a lopsided half-grin. "You shouldn't have gone to see Anderson at his estate! You're dead wrong for going, but the Commish is right. *I* should've reported the call to him. I'm sorry everything turned out like this."

Casey sighed deeply. "Well, now I have a chance to make it right. I promise not to let you down."

"Of course not," he answered. "You have your father's blood in your veins. That's the reason why you're so good at what you do."

And with that, he departed.

Time to get the place back in order.

Casey surveyed her living room. There was blood all over the floor where Tiny's body fell. Amidst all the confusion, she hadn't even noticed that the easy chair closest to the kitchen was overturned.

She took her time, hoping it would help take her mind off things. The superintendent on duty came to put up her new door. The officers outside her apartment didn't let him pass when he got there until she vouched for him. Once she did, they watched him closely, but otherwise they stayed out of the way. The entire time he was there, he never once asked Casey what happened. He knew she was a cop, and if she didn't volunteer any information, then he didn't need to know.

Once he was gone, she took a seat on the sofa. Physically, she felt much better. But she was still too angry and frustrated. Her exercises helped a lot, but she still needed to vent. There was only one person she could talk to.

Cameron, please be home, please be home! Casey thought, mouthing the words as she reached for her cell. To her surprise, it was undamaged in the scuffle. She dialed his number and let out an overwhelming sigh of relief when he picked up.

"Well, this is a nice surprise," Cameron playfully mocked. "Since when do you call me twice in the same day?"

"I *really* need to talk to you." Casey answered him. "I need you to brace yourself. If you're not sitting right now, you should."

After about ten seconds of silence on his end of the line, he finally replied, "Okay, um…I'd call you out for being dramatic, but *you* don't do dramatics. So, let me ask you one question first. Does this involve our last conversation about finding LeAnn?"

"It involves all of us!" Casey spit out the words like a mouthful of salt water. "It involves you, me, LeAnn, and especially mom and dad! It involves what happened the night they were killed, and I feel like I'm going to explode!"

"Why do I feel like you're going to tell me something that'll have me on the red-eye to Saturn City?" he asked. There was no mockery or sarcasm in his voice. "Casey, what's going on?"

"Let's start with why my boss came by after he gave me the day off. Do you remember how we had to cut our conversation short?"

"That does ring a bell, yes."

"My boss stopped by to pass along a message from Shawn Anderson. The turd left a personal invitation for me to come to his mansion, but I wasn't there to receive it."

"And your captain intercepted it," Cameron replied slowly, with a hint of dread in his voice. "I've heard you mention Shawn Anderson to me in the past. Isn't he one of the biggest crime bosses in your city?"

"He's *the* crime boss. Once my Captain left, I decided to find out what Anderson wanted with me, with my gun at the ready, just in case. I should've used my head. I could've ignored the invitation, but I didn't. It was a stupid move. I know that now."

"Casey, I don't like where this is going. But go on."

"I finally met Anderson face-to-face for the very first time." She continued. "In short, it turned out to be a personal recruiting mission. He wanted me to join him, and become his inside man, or woman, rather, in the CIOC. When I refused, he told me he made a similar offer to dad years ago. His bosses wanted our father out of the way, so Anderson tried to recruit him. That inspired Dad to create the CIOC unit to take down the mob, and then Anderson had him murdered."

As Casey expected, Cameron didn't respond right away. He was probably reliving that dreadful night in his head, replaying every detail in slow motion. There was silence on both ends of the line for what felt like a lifetime. She waited patiently for him to process the news she dumped into his lap. She expected an "I told you so" to fly out of his mouth when she told him about the bounty on her head.

"I'm going to draw the obvious conclusion," he finally said. The uneasy tone in his voice didn't seem any more intense than it was before. "Shawn Anderson put out a hit on you, didn't he?"

"A million-dollar hit," Casey answered him. "I'll spare you the full play-by-play, but three people already tried to cash in, two of whom are now in police custody. The other guy was a confirmed cop-killer. He was shot to death by three other members of my unit, right in my living room. I just spent the last two hours cleaning up blood, my apartment door had to be replaced—"

"You're going after him, aren't you?" He cut her off. "Your unit is going after him for what he's done. Is that where this is leading?"

Even though he wasn't physically in the room with her, she nodded. "That's why I called you, Cameron. Like I said, I feel like I'm going to explode, and I need you to talk me through this. I've never felt rage like this before, and I promised Captain Burrell I'd play it his way and do this by the book. But if it does come down to me and that murderous sociopath, I just might put him in the ground."

"So, after all these years…," he said. There was anger in his voice as he spoke. "Now we know. And while I can't speak for LeAnn, because we haven't found her, you and I could've turned out a lot worse. That's what'll be Anderson's downfall. *You* turned out for the better, regardless of what he's done. You're not the eight-year-old kid I hid in dad's panic room with that night.

"If mom and dad were alive, they'd be damn proud of the person you've become. You can't be bought, bullied, or intimidated. Just like dad. That's why Shawn Anderson put a bounty on your head when you refused his offer. He's afraid of you, because you remind him of our father.

"It's why you're so good at your job," he concluded. His deep voice was stern and enthusiastic. All the anger in his tone was completely gone. "And it's why *you're* going to take him down. Because you're Richard Vice's daughter. Show him what that means."

Umm…wow! Casey thought to herself, as she processed what he said. Something familiar about it resonated with her. It was something Captain Burrell said to her right before he left:

You have your father's blood in your veins. That's the reason why you're so good at what you do.

She replayed his "pep-talk" in her head. His words weighed

on her conscience and reinforced her resolve.

"I can do this now," she said, more so to herself than to him. "I can finish what dad started, without it being personal." She stopped to think about it some more, and then said, "Thank you, Cameron. I owe you one, especially for not saying 'I told you so!' This really helped a lot."

"You don't have to thank me for doing the right thing," he replied. "And I don't like that it turned out I was right. Just be careful, kid. And make sure you come back alive! I expect to see you in one piece when this is all over. We'll pick up where we left off with our search for LeAnn. Hopefully we'll finally make some progress."

"Sounds like a plan," she replied. "I've got to head to the office. I'll talk to you soon, hopefully under better circumstances."

"Looking forward to it. Talk to you soon," Cameron said, and then hung up.

Casey closed her eyes and repeated her breathing exercise. She reflected on everything that transpired, from the meeting at the estate to the conversation with her brother. As she combed through every detail in her mind, she felt different. The feelings were still there, and they were intense. But now they wouldn't undermine her judgment. She could finally *control* them.

Now, I'm ready to go.

Chapter 5

Casey gripped the wheel of the armored SUV and brought the vehicle up to 60 mph. Her eyes were fixed on the road ahead, but she managed to steal a quick glance of Giselle and Jonathan in the back seat, then at Burrell, who agreed to ride shotgun. None of them said a word. They just looked at her with identical expressions– cocked eyes and a disapproving scowl.

"My bad, you guys," she said to the three of them. She eased up on the gas and gave the brakes a gentle push. The vehicle slowed down to 30 mph, and Captain Burrell sighed in relief.

"Yeah, we'll get to the rendezvous point soon enough," Burrell said to her over several breaths. "Besides, the two mutts we have in custody told me Anderson has a meeting tonight. He isn't going anywhere. So, stop driving like you're in a Ferrari."

"*They* told you he has a meeting?" Casey asked, giggling. Once she could finally stop, she asked, "How would *they* know?"

"They've been to a few," Burrell replied. "Anderson has them when he has a job or two lined up. He's going to meet with all his underbosses tonight. Each one of them will bring their lieutenants. The estate gets locked down and the butlers, maids, security, etc. are given the night off. The stereotypical, classified mafia stuff."

"And you believed them?" Casey asked. She shook her head. "You don't think it sounds a little too convenient?"

"I agree, but so far their information checks out," Burrell countered. "Our surveillance team reported 39 people arrived at the Anderson estate within the last hour. The personal tail I assigned to him confirmed Shawn Anderson hasn't left his estate in the past five hours."

"That's a lot of guns and muscle," Casey said. She thought about it, and then said, "That doesn't account for Wyatt, Yovanni and Danielle. Do we have a fix on them?"

Her captain nodded. "They were spotted with Anderson the last time he returned to the estate, and they haven't been spotted leaving since. All three of them fit the descriptions you gave, and we ran their names through the database. It's definitely them."

"What about the ones who tried to kill me?" Casey asked. "Where *do* they fit into all of this, aside from the obvious?"

"That's it exactly." Burrell answered her. "After you met with Anderson, he put the word out. One million solid on Casey Vice, preferably dead. The three of them saw their opportunity. They planned to kill you and then collect the reward at the meeting."

Yeah. And how'd that work out for em'? "Why are we coordinating the mission out of an abandoned cul-de-sac, a mile away from Anderson's estate?" She asked him.

"It was the commissioner's direct order," Burrell explained. "He isn't taking any chances after the attempt on your life. We're doing this mission as far under the radar as possible. Until the mission is accomplished, it's on the books as a routine training exercise."

"I like how he thinks," Casey said with a nod. "Anderson has less of a chance of being tipped off, *and* he'll never see us coming until it's too late. That's good."

"Speaking of whom," Burrell said, as he delivered a playful tap on her shoulder, "I met with the Judge to get the arrest warrant signed, right? And I'm telling you, his smile was wide enough that I thought his ears would fall off. He snatched the warrant out of my hand at the sound of Anderson's name. I burst out laughing in front of his wife, I couldn't help it."

Once she, Jonathan and Giselle finally stopped laughing, Casey responded, "Cap, that doesn't sound like you at all. But hey, in our line of work, you take a feel-good moment when and where you can get one, right?"

"Amen Hallelujah to that!" Burrell said with a smile.

The rest of the ride continued in silence. Casey made a swift turn into the cul-de-sac and parked behind one of the SWAT trucks. Casey's unit wore the letters "CIOC" across their helmets and vests. Her own detective insignia consisted of two inverted silver chevrons with a small silver diamond underneath.

Unlike the others, Casey didn't carry her regular Taser this time, or even a rifle. She pulled her two black Ruger P95PR pistols from their carry case, assembled them, and holstered them to either side of her waist. She reached into the carry case for the spare magazines and shoved them into the pouches of her pants.

Afterwards, she took out her personal pair of Firefly Blast Knuckles and double-checked the lithium batteries in each one. Normally used by less traditional martial artists, the stunners packed over 900,000 volts behind every punch. Should the opportunity arise for *her* to apprehend the target and he decided to go down swinging, a semi-automatic wasn't going to grant the kind of closure she wanted before she put him in handcuffs.

Orders or no orders, the fool is still going to suffer. Casey clipped the stunners to her belt. Dressed, armed and ready to go, she made her way to the second SWAT truck and approached Captain Burrell.

"Cap, how're we looking so far?" she asked once she got within earshot.

The broad-shouldered man turned to her and nodded. "We have all of the muscle to pull this off, plus a surprise or two in reserve." He gestured to the small pile of papers in front of him. "Come take a look at this."

Casey moved in close and looked at the pile of papers. Her mouth flew open when she realized what they were. Captain Burrell burst out laughing.

"These are..." she said, the rest of her sentence caught in her throat. Her eyes met Captain Burrell's, and she asked, "How did you get the blueprints to Shawn Anderson's estate?"

"I cashed in a last-minute favor with an old friend." Burrell explained. "I want you to go over these blueprints during the mission brief. Point out anything you believe will give us the advantage."

"I didn't see a whole lot while I was there, but I'll do my best."

"That's all I ask," Captain Burrell said with a brief nod. He handed her a pen from his pocket and called out, "Alright everyone! Gather round!"

The entire taskforce moved in haste toward the back of the SWAT truck. Whispers traveled through the group as they huddled up. Casey noted the eagerness in their faces as they moved into a circle.

"We all know why we're here," Captain Burrell began to explain. He raised his voice just loud enough for everyone in the group to hear. "Shawn Anderson, the biggest crime boss in our city, attempted to recruit one of our own into his ranks. Then he *tried* and *failed* to have her killed when she declined the offer.

"Our orders are to bring him in alive," he continued. "Our source confirmed that he's locked up in his mansion with the biggest players in his criminal regime. They're *all* well-armed and extremely dangerous. But this is our best chance to cut off the head of the mafia and I refuse to pass it up."

"Tell it like it is!" One of the SWAT team members shouted over the various cheers of the taskforce. Many of them clapped in agreement, but a stern hand held high in the air by Winston Dodds, the SWAT team's lead sergeant, silenced the entire group.

Burrell cleared his throat and continued, "We'll divide the CIOC and SWAT teams evenly. Half of each team will form up with me as team one, the assault team. We'll converge on the property from the front. Our objective is to get to the primary suspect as quickly as possible, but I want the react team to move into position *first*.

"The remaining half will form team two, the react team, under Sergeant Dodds. You will converge on the estate from the rear and cover team one. Wait until we've engaged the enemy. Subdue all resistance, but the fewer the casualties, the better." His attention briefly turned to Casey. "Are you ready, Detective?"

Casey gave Burrell a nod and then turned to the blueprints. She overlaid the mental image of Anderson's safe room with its corresponding location, and then looked up to address the entire group once she was ready.

Her index finger gently brushed underneath her lower lip. After a few seconds, she said, "They have a better chance to organize themselves inside of the mansion. So, we need to force them outside and fight us on *our* terms. Our assault team can use the SWAT trucks as battering rams to breach the front gate."

"That should make a loud enough ruckus to draw *almost* everyone out," Burrell added with a narrow grin. "*They* would have to come to *us*. We can use the SWAT trucks and *their* vehicles as cover when they start shooting. Then the react team can flank them from the rear with less resistance."

"What did you mean by *almost* everyone?" Sergeant Dodds asked him.

"Exactly what he said," Casey replied. "See this room right here?" She asked, and circled the room labeled "guest suite" on the layout for the second floor. "It's been rebuilt it into a panic room. If it's anything like I've seen before, it's bulletproof, and it locks from the *inside*. Take out Anderson's guys before he can make it to that room.

"There are also three high-profile individuals to watch out for." She continued. "First, there's Wyatt, Shawn Anderson's right-hand stooge. I'm certain he'll be the one to organize the troops. That leaves Anderson's personal bodyguards: Yovanni and Danielle. If Wyatt is outside fighting us, they'll be *inside* guarding the boss. We won't get anywhere near that room, if either of them can help it."

"Or within reach of Anderson," Captain Burrell said. With a slight shake of his head, he rubbed his chin and added, "Either we get them to surrender or we take them down. Then it's just him, panic room or no panic room. If even *one* of us can get to him…" he paused, took a deep breath, and continued, "…it's a chance we have to take, because we're not leaving empty handed. Let's roll out!"

Casey hurried into the passenger seat of the nearest SWAT truck. Burrell immediately climbed into the driver seat and started it up. Within minutes they were within view of the mansion, and Burrell brought the truck to a stop.

"Team One Leader, this is the Team Two Leader. Do you copy?" called the raspy voice of Sergeant Dodds over the field radio.

Burrell leaned his head toward his radio and answered, "Copy, Team Two Leader. This is Team One Leader. What's your twenty?"

A few seconds of radio silence passed before the Sergeant replied, "We've successfully breached the rear gate of the estate. So far, there's been no response from the inside. We are clear to move into position, on your command."

"Copy that. We're in position, three hundred feet away," Burrell said, nodding to himself. "Stay mindful of potential hostiles. Team One Leader out."

Five minutes later, the radio buzzed to life, and the Sergeant's voice whispered, "Team One Leader, this is Team Two Leader.

We are in position. I repeat: Team Two is in position. Do you copy, Team One Leader?"

"I copy, Sergeant. How many hostiles can you put eyes on?" Burrell asked.

"Team One leader, we can confirm 40 hostiles on the ground level, but we can't put our eyes on the Prize," Dodds whispered in haste. "I repeat: 40 hostiles accounted for so far, but the Prize is nowhere in sight."

"I'll bet you a month's pay he's already in that room." Casey snapped. "Cap, there's no point in waiting. We have to strike now."

Burrell's slammed his fist against the steering wheel. With radio in hand, he snapped, "Team Two Leader, copy that. We're on the move! Team One, this is Team One Leader. Move in! Breach the perimeter! I repeat: Breach the perimeter, *now*!"

Yes! Drive this clunker like it's a damn Ferrari! Casey thought, as Burrell slammed his boot on the accelerator with a threatening grunt. She pressed her back against the seat as the truck continued to gain speed, and within less than a minute, the forward perimeter of the Anderson estate was within reach. Casey yelled "Everyone brace for impact!" and clenched her jaw as the truck collided with the mansion's wrought iron gates.

The heavily reinforced vehicle won out. Captain Burrell eased off the gas and hit the brakes as he steered hard to the right. As his side of the truck struck three Sedans parked along the front yard, combat-tested reinforced alloy trumped factory-tested metal and fiberglass.

Casey grasped the overhead grip as the behemoth vehicle continued its rampage, until they stopped two feet from the garage on the right side of the house. The resounding clash on the opposite side of the yard brought a smile to her face. She undid her seatbelt and hurried out of her side of the truck. Burrell followed behind her as their teammates poured out from the rear of the truck posthaste.

"Everyone get into position!" Burrell ordered, gripping his field radio.

Casey reached for her gun and positioned herself between the front of the truck and the side of the garage. The gap between them provided her with sufficient cover *and* a good view of the mansion's front entryway.

Here they come. She thought to herself as the front door flew open.

A small stampede of casually dressed men, armed with pistols, rifles and shotguns, made their way into the front yard.

They stopped short of the few vehicles that hadn't been violated by the Assault Team's abrupt entrance and spat out blasphemous obscenities of every kind in response to the chaos.

"Damn coppahs!" One of the men shouted. "These damn coppahs done lost their effin' mahbles! Look at this crap!"

"Wyatt! You see 'dis?" Another of them called out. "The Jackknife is gonna be pissed!"

"He ain't gonna have to deal with 'dis!" Wyatt called out, as he stepped into the yard. "Because *we're* gonna! Isn't that right, *Vice?!* This crazy, reckless bee-ess has *you* written all over it! So, you're still alive after all! You think you gettin' even tonight, girlie? Well, guess *what*?! That ain't hap'nin! B'cause you and your coppah friends are dead!"

Casey shook her head. *You could at least speak proper English, you illiterate putz!*

"I don't think they're very happy," Burrell's voice whispered over Casey's shoulder. "They seem a little pissed off, don't you think?"

"Boys, we got unwelcomed guests. Get out here, now!" Wyatt continued to yell, with an Uzi in his hands and a cock-eyed scowl across his face. "Vice is still alive, so the bounty is still hot! Grab the gear and light em' up. I want to see a *body* for Casey Vice. *No exceptions*!"

Casey didn't turn to face Burrell, but through the corner of her eye she caught his mischievous grin. She smiled in response and whispered, "*Now,* you know what *my* life is like! Welcome to Maverick Cop University! I'll teach you everything you need to know, but it's a '*learn fast or die'* curriculum. You either get an 'A', or you fail the course."

Burrell fought the urge to laugh, and nodded playfully, "We'll have to skip the Indoc, *and* the Grand Tour! Let's get to the good part, shall we?"

Casey turned to face him and smiled. "Cap, you just *might* make the Honor Roll!"

"It would be the first time in my life, ya know?" Burrell said with a smile, as he grabbed his radio and whispered, "Team Two Leader, this is Team One Leader. We've flushed the rats out of the hole. We're gonna draw their fire and subdue as many as we can.

"I want you to wait until *after* they start shooting, *and then* call for the police chopper," he continued. He ignored the wide-eyed look on Casey's face, and added, "You and your team will move in *after* you get the affirmative from the Air Support

Team. Unless you encounter a hostile, standby and let Team One take all the heat until the helicopter arrives. Spitfire and I will get their attention. Team One, be ready to cover us."

"We're in position across the main entrance," Jonathan said softly over the radio. "Let's cook it up!"

"Copy that," Giselle's voice whispered over the radio. "We're in position on this end, and we're ready to go."

"That's a tall order, Captain," Sergeant Dodds replied in a hushed tone, "But roger that. *Please*, don't take any unnecessary risks."

Burrell shook his head. "No promises. Team One Leader out."

"A *helicopter?!*" Casey said, with no audible sound to the words as she mouthed them. "Even I didn't think you…ooh! The *surprise* or two you mentioned during the briefing. Oh, you're *good*!"

"Learn fast or die, right?" Burrell whispered with a grin. "Okay, here we go!

"Ready," Casey nodded, and followed him to the tail end of the truck. She stopped when she was within Wyatt's direct line of sight. Burrell took a firm grip onto the back of her Kevlar vest. She took aim above her head, fired a shot and yelled, "SCPD!"

She stumbled into Burrell when he yanked hard on her vest, just a millisecond before a mass discharge of bullets lit up the spot where she *had been* standing. Several rounds grazed the armor-plating of the truck, but none of them hit her.

"Waste that broad!" she heard Wyatt shout over the rain of ammunition that cut through the air. "Kill the dogs! Fifty grand extra for every dead cop. Anyone who lets a badge get pass them, I'll shoot you myself! Ignore the damage to the cars and keep shooting, dammit! Kill em' all!"

"Everyone fire at will!" Burrell shouted. He turned to Casey and asked, "You get your footing back yet?"

"Yeah, thanks. I've got a plan," Casey replied, she gestured towards the garage and headed that way, towards the front end of the truck. As Burrell followed her, she said, "There's just enough space over here to run past these idiots while Air Support distracts them, after the React Team moves in. We'll get a miniscule window of opportunity for one of us to get into the house. Whoever it is will have to pick off a few chumps on the way in, but—"

Burrell shook his head. "That's a lot of heat for one person to put on themselves, especially since every cop out here has a price on their head. Still, I did say I wasn't leaving empty handed."

"Let me do it." Casey nodded to Burrell. "I know you want Anderson alive, but if we can't get to him before these fools get lucky and pick us off…" She paused, and then added, "It's either *him* or *us*. That's how I see it. I'll keep my promise to do this *your* way. I *will* make it my priority to arrest him *first*, if I'm the only one who can get inside."

A volley of bullets pelted the front of the truck on the opposite side. Wyatt continued to shout over the gunfire, but Casey ignored his unintelligent, slanderous taunts.

"I hear you, kid." Burrell nodded and raised his voice over the orchestra of semi-automatic weapons, so she could hear him. "But what you're suggesting is suicide! Even if you could get past them, it would be by the skin of your teeth. And then there's the panic room, the two bodyguards we haven't seen yet…"

Casey arched an eyebrow. "When the opportunity presents itself, we'll be out of time. Just *make* the decision *now* so there's no second-guessing it when the time comes. I'll follow your lead."

Burrell opened his mouth to respond, but the bright lights and chuffing hum of rotary blades interrupted him.

"This is Commissioner Oleander of the Saturn City Police!" shouted the robust voice over a megaphone. "You're *all* under arrest for complicity in an attempted capital murder! Now drop your guns, get on your knees and put your hands behind your heads!"

"Screw you, you ol' piece-a-crap!" One of the mobsters shouted irreverently over the jeers of several of his peers. "Shoot em' down!"

As they raised their weapons towards the helicopter, they were cut down by Sergeant Dodds and his React Team, who made their way into the front yard from the left side.

So much for fewer casualties, Casey thought. She turned to Captain Burrell and said, "It's now or never, Cap. What's your call?"

"I ain't gonna like this, but…" Burrell shook his head, glanced at the chaos ahead of them, returned his gaze to Casey, and gave her a quick nod. "…go. We'll cover you and follow you in as fast as we can. Just *stay alive*, whatever it takes."

Casey smiled and reached for her second gun. She squeezed between the grill of the SWAT truck and the garage, and took aim on Wyatt, who turned towards her just as she broke from cover. Six rounds caught him in the leg, chest, and abdomen. She refused to break her stride to watch him hit the ground and broke into a sprint past four more mobsters as they were gunned down by the Air Support Team.

She made it to the front door within seconds, then spun around and fired on two of Jackknife's Lieutenants. Her attention turned to her Captain, who suffered a gunshot to the arm. From the grin on his face, it wasn't anything serious. Their eyes met for an instant, and he nodded towards the direction of the house. She obliged with a nod, mouthed the words *"stay alive, whatever it takes"* and ran inside.

Chapter 6

Casey disappeared into the empty dining room to her left, pistols drawn and ready. As she went over the details of mansion's layout in her mind, the elevator directly across the adjoining hallway grabbed her attention.

No, that isn't a good idea, especially if I get ambushed. I'll take the stairs instead.

She charged into the hallway and ascended the stairs to the right. To her surprise, she hadn't encountered anyone. As she made it to the top, her attention turned toward the room to her left.

Yeah, they're in there, alright. I'll have to get Danielle and Yovanni out of the way, before I can get to Anderson. Fortunately, I've got a million-dollar price tag on my life. If they knew it was me out here…

Casey raised her gun above her head, fired a round, and yelled, "So, um, does anyone *else* want a chance to make a million dollars?"

The door opened five seconds later, and both Yovanni and Danielle emerged from the room. Casey kept both guns pointed at their heads as they shut the door behind them.

"The love of money really *is* the root of all evil," Casey spat out, as she shook her head. She nodded at their weapons. "You don't need those guns or batons. I'm not going to let you use them, so *lose* em'. Now."

Neither of them moved.

Casey fired a single shot that missed Yovanni's ear by a hairsbreadth. All the color drained from their faces, and Casey nodded towards the end of the balcony, on their far right.

"That's your only warning," She hissed in a low, even voice, and refocused her pistol on Yovanni's forehead. "Now, then. Weapons, please. I will not tell you again."

Danielle immediately reached for both of her guns and hurled them across the hall towards the elevator. She frantically reached for her baton and tossed it, then raised both hands in the air.

"This is *all your* fault, you know," Yovanni snapped, as she threw her guns aside. She unstrapped her baton from her leg, tossed it, and spit out, "Why couldn't you just take the Jackknife's offer?!"

"Shawn Anderson had my father killed when I was eight years old," Casey admitted. Her voice was calm, but she kept her guns aimed at their foreheads as she spoke. "My mother was caught in the crossfire, and I lost both of my parents in one night. I was only *eight years old*, Yovanni. My older brother was 12. My little sister was five. *Five*!

"That's who the two of you work for," she continued. "A despot who orphans children and *still* gets to sleep every night. That's how you make your living. In service to a shameless, depraved lunatic who only cares about himself."

Yovanni's shook her head, and her eyes teared up. "I didn't know. I mean, I know your father was murdered years ago, but I didn't know *he* was responsible. I'm sorry."

"No, you're not." Casey shook her head. "I realize neither of you will give up your boss, but I don't *need* or *want* your deaths on my conscience. So, you get one chance to *walk* away. I suggest you take it."

"Really?! You're just letting us go?" Yovanni asked, as she wiped the tears from her eyes.

Casey shrugged in response without lowering her guns. "Hey, you're not off the hook," she warned her, and tilted her head towards the foyer below. "Can you hear that? Your 'family' is dying because they chose loyalty over staying alive. Be smarter than them. Turn yourselves in, and *my* people *will* make it worth your while."

Danielle and Yovanni exchanged looks, then hurried down the left stairwell.

That went better than I hoped, Casey nodded to herself, as she lowered her guns. *Now how do I get into the room?*

An abrupt discharge of bullets echoed from the foyer below, one of which grazed her left arm. She cried out as pain lanced through her limb and turned to see three of Jackknife's men ascend the staircase behind her. They took aim and unleashed another volley as they reached the balcony.

Casey dove for cover by the elevator in the hallway to the far left and stayed as low as possible to avoid getting shot through the wall. With a steady grip on her weapons, she pushed the pain out of her mind as the shooters continued to unload. Chunks of wood and sheetrock from the walls shattered and fell to the floor around her, and her helmet was pelted by debris. Twenty seconds later, the familiar *tick and click* of emptied semi-automatic weapons signaled a small reprieve.

"That's my cue! Gotta make it count!" She whispered. She speedily emerged from her cover and let loose a relentless burst of gunfire. All three men hit the balcony floor in a heap, as multiple shots to the chest and head brought their lives to a swift end.

A quick survey of the vicinity confirmed she was out of immediate danger. Casey ejected the clips from both guns and re-loaded them with fresh mags. Then she walked over to the bodies and checked them over. One of them had a frag grenade clipped to his belt, and her lips formed a closed, cruel smile…

Yep, that'll do nicely! Such a thoughtful fellow, aren't ya?

"Thanks, handsome," Casey mocked, and grabbed the grenade from his corpse. She hurried to the door, got down on one knee and held the grenade against it. She pulled the pin, made a break for the hallway between the elevator and the neighboring bedroom, and coved her ears. She felt the vibration of the blast as the explosion rung through the house.

She rushed toward the panic room to find that the door hadn't been blown off. The blast weakened the structure enough to kick the door open, and Casey braced herself. With a stiff straight kick, the door hit the adjacent wall with a thunderous smack.

With pistol firmly in hand, Casey slowly stepped into the room. From her initial vantage point, there was nothing special about the room. There were three doors: one to the terrace, one to the bathroom, and one more that led to a walk-in closet. The prime suspect, however, was nowhere in sight…

"Shawn Anderson! This is SCPD!" Casey yelled, her gun aimed at the closet door. She walked over to the large desk in the middle of the room and peaked behind it. Then she aimed her gun at the bathroom door, and said, "You're under arrest for orchestrating a capital murder."

The room remained silent.

"I know you're in here, Jackknife!" She snapped, before adding, "One way or another, I'm gonna bring you in. Now come out with your hands–"

The closet door flew open.

Casey's head spun to the left a millisecond too late. The butt of a .44 handgun landed hard on her chin, and she hit the hardwood floor like a boulder. She coughed violently as Shawn Anderson brought his right foot down on her chest twice.

"Did you like that, *Vice*?" Anderson shouted, as he strode toward her in triumph. He aimed the revolver at her and kicked her gun across the room. Spit flew out of his mouth as he shouted, "I offered you mercy! A chance to be somebody! And *this* is how you repay me?"

Casey struggled to ignore the throbbing pain in her jaw, left arm and chest as she rolled out of Anderson's line of fire. She kicked him in the stomach, and he lost his balance–and his gun. The revolver sailed across the floor, towards the terrace door. Anderson scrambled back to his feet and hurried to retrieve it.

Oh, no you don't! Casey groggily took off after her target and kicked him in the groin before he reached his gun. The crotch shot dropped him to his knees, and Casey, refusing to touch his gun, kicked it towards the desk in the middle of the room.

"Did you like *that*, Anderson?" She mocked. She backed up towards the desk, just a few feet from the gun. *To hell if I let you catch me by surprise a second time!* She watched Anderson intently as he slowly got back to his feet, his expression even more viscous than before.

"You've got a huge set of brass ones on you, don't you, Red?" Anderson snapped. He looked behind her, probably to where she kicked his gun, and added, "You have the nerve to think you can take me on by yourself? I'll kill you with my bare hands, you little punk!"

So predictable, Casey thought. *You've had this coming since the night my parents were murdered. I made a promise not to murder you outright, but I'm gonna make sure you suffer before I put you in handcuffs.*

Casey ducked underneath his wild swings. She landed several

lightning fast jabs to his stomach. Anderson staggered backward towards the wall. Casey gave chase and caught him on the jaw with a stiff left cross. Despite her injury, Anderson's head whipped back from the sheer force. She continued to land one punch after another, but Anderson was *still* standing.

The larger man rushed at her in a fit of rage, and she took a hard punch to the stomach. Another punch to the chest sent her to the ground. The impact with which she landed knocked most of the air out of her lungs and her Kevlar helmet off of her head.

"I was a golden gloves champion in my youth, little girl," the large man told her. He stood confidently, grinning at her as she doubled over. "Did you *really* think *you* could beat *me* one-on-one in a fistfight?"

You shouldn't have let up. Stupid! I won't make the same mistake. Casey quickly put on the blast knuckles and turned them on. She dashed toward him and caught him with a straight punch to the right side of his head. He howled as the intense voltage forced him back against the wall.

He tried to cover up, but it was ultimately in vain. Her own pain fueled her rage as she pressed her offensive, throwing unorthodox combinations of hooks, jabs and haymakers to his head and body. The voltage, power, and speed behind her attacks left him completely helpless as she continued to pummel him.

Battered, groggy, and stubborn, yet still unwilling to admit defeat, Anderson recklessly reached out to grab her by the arms, aiming directly for the wound on her upper left arm. When he finally managed to get ahold of the flesh wound, a sudden surge of adrenaline spurred her on. She stepped in and threw a left kick to his gut, forcing him to let go as he struggled to catch his breath. She put the steel toe of her boots to work as she landed kicks to his ribs and his back. Then she put all her weight on her left leg and delivered a side kick to the gut that knocked him to his knees. He broke into a coughing fit, spitting up blood and saliva as he tried to get back up, throwing up his hand in surrender.

Having finally subdued him, she turned off her stun knuckles and put them back on her belt. She could feel the adrenaline wearing off as she reached for her handcuffs and her gun. Fatigue set in; she could feel the pain in her body from the thrashing she'd taken. Her left arm was almost completely numb, but she wasn't bleeding. Her jaw, abdomen and chest were aching. Fortunately, it could have been a lot worse. She could've been him: bruised, bloody, and humiliated.

"I'm taking you in, Anderson." she declared, watching him wipe the blood from his mouth. "I may not be able to prove you had my parents murdered…yet, but you're going to do time for putting a hit out on me."

"You're going to have to kill me first!" He yelled in a fit of rage, as he pulled his gun and took aim.

Dammit, Casey! She'd been too focused on stomping Anderson into submission; she hadn't realized how close he was to the revolver. She'd kicked the weapon away from him before their brawl, but her need for self-satisfaction got the best of her. She didn't even notice that he'd picked it up.

Time seemed to slow down in that moment. On pure instinct, Casey drew her own weapon, took aim, and fired two shots straight to his heart. Anderson shuddered as the bullets went through him. Blood rushed from the exit wounds in his back as he fell backwards onto his desk.

And then time sped back up to normal again.

She walked over to where Anderson's head rested on the desk, with her gun in hand. He wasn't breathing, but his eyes were wide open and lusterless. His grip loosened around his handgun. Casey pressed her index and middle finger against his neck. There was no pulse. Shawn Anderson, the man who destroyed her family and terrorized her city for more than a decade, was dead.

It's…its over; she thought to herself. Sadness swept over her as she stared at his lifeless form. Even after everything he'd done, she regretted killing him. Even if it was self-defense.

The sound of radio chatter behind her caught her attention, and she turned to see Captain Burrell step into the room. He hadn't said a word. He just looked at her with a somber expression on his face.

Giselle walked into the room seconds later, but she didn't say anything once she saw the look on Burrell's face. Casey moved away from the body and headed towards them in silence. Neither of them moved as she passed by them. The target had been neutralized. Burrell called it in over the radio just as she made it through the door.

Chapter 7

Casey and Burrell debriefed for three hours following the mission, then they treaded through a stack of paperwork for another two before he sent her home. She changed out of her gear, took a long shower and replaced the dressing around the wound to her left arm. The meds given to her by the hospital's EMT finally kicked in, so she wasn't in pain. Only her saddened state of being remained.

She changed into her pajamas, stood at the mirror in the bathroom, and forced an ear-to-ear grin. There was a sadness in her countenance she hadn't seen since the night her parents were murdered.

"That feels awkward," she said out loud and strolled into the living room. "No more forcing myself to smile."

Casey sat on the far end the sofa and grabbed a framed picture on the end table. It was a picture of her and her parents on her eighth birthday, just a few months before they were murdered. She, LeAnn, and their mother shared a similar skin complexion and the same shade of red hair, but her sister had their mother's green eyes. Casey got her eyes from her father.

The man in the photo had very broad features, and his face was less serious in the picture than she remembered. As best as she could recall, he always called out of the office on birthdays, Thanksgiving and Christmas. Any other holiday was negotiable, but those specific occasions weren't open for debate.

Her mother was the kind of person who never had an enemy in her entire life; she was just that loveable. A woman who rarely lost control of her own feelings, she could talk anyone out of a bad mood, and if that didn't work...

Tears poured down Casey's cheeks, some of them dropping onto the glass protecting the picture. Cut off in the middle of her thoughts, she raised her knees to her chest and curled up in her spot on the sofa. She hadn't realized she was crying. The brave, teary-eyed eight-year-old who held the family portrait in her hands on the night that her parents died had been too angry to cry. LeAnn did all the screaming and crying for her, too. Now *she* needed to release the fifteen years of pain bottled up inside of her.

So, for the next five hours, all she did was cry.

When she finally stopped crying, the awkward feelings were gone. She'd finally found the closure she needed. Wiping the tears from her eyes, she noticed that she dropped the picture on the floor while she had been crying. Fortunately, the frame hadn't been broken in the process. She got up out of her seat and picked it up, wiped her tears from it and put it back on the end table where it belonged.

Casey sat back down in the same spot on the couch. There was no point in going to bed; there was no chance of going to asleep. It was already after three in the morning, and she had to be in the office by six-thirty. So instead she just sat there with her eyes closed, focused on her follow-up with Burrell coming up in a few hours and the decision she needed to make.

* * *

Casey walked into Captain Burrell's office, shut the door behind her and waited as he stood at the window across the room. It was one of his daily habits, and Casey knew not to say a word until he was done.

"You look tired, kid," Burrell finally said to her. "Is your left arm feeling any better?"

"It's still a little sore, but I'll be fine," Casey admitted. "The meds the EMT gave me work wonders, but I didn't get any sleep. I was up all night reflecting on what happened."

He spun around to face her. She noted the grin across his face as he looked her over.

"How's *your* arm?" she asked him after she noticed that, like her, his arm wasn't in a sling.

"I've had worse done to me over the years. So, I'll live," Burrell insisted. He motioned to the empty chair directly in front of her. "Grab yourself a seat, kid."

"Thank you, Captain," she replied.

"So, I got a call from the commissioner a half hour ago," he said. "He explained that after Anderson's mansion was searched, they found the recording of the meeting between the two of you, and his confession to the murder of Captain Richard Vice is on there."

Casey smiled. "Will that be enough to…?"

Burrell reciprocated her smile with one of his own. "Secure the DA's approval for an investigation into Anderson's activities over the last 15 to 20 years? Yep."

Casey sat silent as her captain read her expression.

"I know you did your best to bring Anderson in alive," Burrell told her, as he reached for a yellow folder on his desk. "I could tell from the guilt on your face when I finally reached you."

"I gave you my word, and I wanted to deliver," Casey replied. "By the way, what was Oleander's take on Anderson's death? I didn't get to say much to him after the mission."

"Commissioner Oleander loves you to life!" he answered with a grin. "Off the record? He told me if *he'd* made it to Jackknife first, he would've put him down himself. He'd been waiting for an opportunity like this for years, and he said he was glad to help us with air support. He said it made him feel like a SWAT officer again!"

"The helicopter *was* a nice surprise!" She admitted. "I love the Commish! It was good to have him there to back us up. All jokes aside, Cap, we probably wouldn't have pulled that mission of without him."

"I agree. That was the roughest op we've done in a while," Burrell admitted. "It was a good one, though. We didn't lose anyone this time around. A few other members of our taskforce also suffered a few grazes. Sergeant Dodds has a minor flesh wound to the leg, but nothing serious. As for the other side, only two people survived the encounter."

"Yovanni and Danielle."

"They surrendered without incident." Burrell replied. "I was in shock to see them alive *and* unarmed! They ran directly to *me* and said you convinced them to turn themselves in. They've been very cooperative, and the DA is willing to cut them a deal. Well done!"

"I thought it'd be for the best, so I took a chance," Casey said with a shrug. "I'm just happy they have a chance to turn their lives around. It makes it a win for them, even if they don't see it yet."

"Casey, you're growing up! Now, about the section in your report where you explained *how* you got into the panic room. I mean, for real? You used *a hand grenade?!*"

Casey burst out laughing. "Yep!"

"Don't you have the best luck?" Burrell said, laughing. "I can't even picture that in my head, Commando! *How* did you get your hands on a grenade?"

"I took it from one of the mobsters," she admitted with a smile. "I needed to get into the room, and gunfire wasn't going to work. Besides, he was dead, so he didn't need it!"

"No, I suppose he didn't," Burrell replied. "Now, let's get to the real reason I wanted to follow-up with you. I want to know how *you're* doing. You've been through a lot. I need to know if you're okay. So, talk to me. Do you need anything?"

"I need some distance from the job," she replied suddenly. "I don't feel like myself anymore, and I can't function like this. This entire ordeal did something to me. I want to figure out what, and I can't do that here."

Burrell nodded. "You're *finally* going to take a well-deserved, yet long overdue vacation? I'll give you as many as 60 days, if you're interested."

Casey shook her head. "I don't want to take a vacation. When I say I want some distance from the job, I mean I'm officially quitting the Force."

"Casey, you…" Burrell cut himself off, and then asked. "Can you at least take the 60 days off as time to reconsider?"

"There's no need. I've made up my mind." Casey countered. She rose up in her seat and grabbed her gun and her badge. She laid them down on his desk next to each other before Burrell could object any further. As she stood up to leave, he rose from his seat and extended his hand.

"Very well," Burrell said, with sadness in his voice. "I accept your resignation, effective immediately."

Casey reached forward and shook his. "Thank you, Captain. And don't worry; Knowing you, I'm sure I'll see you around sometime."

Giving him one last smile as a gesture of goodbye, she turned and walked out of his office.

Once she finally made it out of the building, she walked until she made it to the bottom of the steps and stopped. She took a moment to pause and reflect; it would be her last time entering and exiting the building as a police officer. A minute later, she made her way down the street with her head held high. It was the end of one chapter in her life, and the beginning of another.

Epilogue

Casey planted herself on the couch, eager to find something worth watching on TV, but admitted defeat after channel-surfing for an hour. She surveyed her apartment for visible signs of what occurred. There were none. The only thing left for her to do was to find a way to move on.

The phone rang, and after a moment of reluctance she checked the caller ID.

A blocked number, huh? Casey shook her head at the caller ID. *Yeah, I'm not gonna bother. Especially after everything I just went through.*

The phone continued to ring. Casey's head continued to shake, her arms folded across her chest.

Logic whispered in her ear: *Answer the damn phone. Listen to your instincts and stop listening to your feelings all the time. Your feelings lie more often than you'll let yourself believe. You can always hang up if the call turns out to be a waste of time.*

Halfway through the fifth ring, Casey picked up the receiver.

"Good morning."

"Indeed it is, Miss Vice," the caller replied with excitement in his voice. "My apologies, but I am speaking to Cassandra Vice, correct?" The man had a Scottish accent. Casey couldn't a recall any Scottish person she might have ties to.

"Umm, yes you are," Casey answered hesitantly. "Who am I speaking to, if you don't mind my asking?"

"For now, you may address me as 'the Commandant'," he answered with a hint of dramatic pause.

Commandant of *what!?* Casey exploded with laughter, and playfully asked, "Is that your real name?"

"In my organization, that's my rank," he admitted.

"That's your *rank*," she repeated. Casey fought the urge to hang up, and asked, "Well then, Mr. Commandant, what exactly can I do for you?"

"I'm glad to have caught your interest," he said. "You see, Miss Vice, I've followed your whole career. From your first bust as a beat cop to your recent dismemberment of the mafia."

Casey's heart skipped a beat, and she bit her bottom lip. *I checked the news channels when I came home. That information isn't public knowledge yet. Aside from the judge, the commissioner, and the taskforce, no one knew about the mission.*

There's no way he should know about that.

One of the reasons why the CIOC unit was so effective is because no one is privy to the unit's activities. Only with the commissioner's authorization can information be divulged to the public after the missions are complete. It prevented leaks and maximized their mission success. Captain Burrell and the commissioner would keep everything quiet until the commissioner was ready to approach the media with answers.

"Where did you hear that?" she asked, neither admitting nor denying anything. "It might be dangerous for you to have that kind of information."

"I have friends in places where most people usually don't," he explained. "Besides, danger comes with the territory in my line of work, so I'll take my chances. In fact, *I'm* taking a chance by reaching out to you."

"Taking a chance on *me*, huh?" Casey asked. *Seriously, like, what the hell do you want?* She exhaled in surrender, and asked, "Okay, I'll bite. What exactly *is* your line of work?

"I'm glad you asked," the man said excitedly. "I'm the director of a covert agency that operates on a global scale, far under the radar of any government. We are comprised of extraordinary individuals, trained to handle 'extraordinary situations' that no one else can, with legal jurisdiction in every major country in the world."

"So, you're a spy?"

"No, I'm not a spy, Miss Vice," he answered plainly.

Still can't get a fix on him, she blew out her breath again, and asked, "Well, what the hell does your *elite* agency *want* with *me*?"

"I'm going to recruit you, Miss Vice," he answered, more confidently than she liked. "You successfully dismantled the mafia over the last three years. That credential alone sets you apart from the average person. I need you, your unorthodox skills and tactics."

Casey remained silent. She nodded to herself. *The convenience of his call seems too well-timed. He does sound like an honest man, though. Like an honest, well-educated, elderly, Scottish man in his late sixties.*

She inhaled deeply, and asked, "An elderly, Scottish man is calling me from a blocked number, to recruit me into a covert organization? Conveniently after I *just quit my job*?"

"I can understand your reluctance," he said in an even tone. There was no excitement in his voice anymore. "But you *do* need a job. And I need *you* because things are going to happen in the not-*too*-distant future. You have a *special* part to play, Miss Vice."

"So, this is all just a matter of common interest?" she asked. "I could just as easily find another job elsewhere—"

"I'm sure you could," he cut her off. "But what if I make a gesture of good faith? You see, I'm aware of your failed attempts to find your younger sister, LeAnn Vice. The manner in which I know this is not important. But, in exchange for you joining my organization, what if I found her for you?"

Casey's heart drummed rapidly in her chest at the sound of LeAnn's name. After six years of running in circles with Cameron, this man offered to do what Casey and her brother could not, to put what's left of her family back together.

"This is all a bit much. I need a few days to think this over," she finally said. "For now, I'll keep this call between the two of us. I'm sorting through a few things right now."

"Naturally," he answered her. "But give me your word that you'll at least think about it."

"Okay, you have my word," she agreed. "How do I get in contact with you?"

"You don't," he countered dryly. "*I'll* contact *you* in three days."

Casey flinched, and then nodded. "I look forward to hearing from you in three days."

She hung up the phone, leaned back on the sofa, and assessed the phone call in her head.

It does sound a little too good to be true, logic whispered in her ear, *but something about him seems genuine. As elusive as he is, it wouldn't hurt to at least consider the proposition, especially if he really can find LeAnn. Just remember to keep your guard up but also keep an open mind.*

"That settle's it then," Casey exclaimed to herself.

-The End-